# The Boy and the Dragon

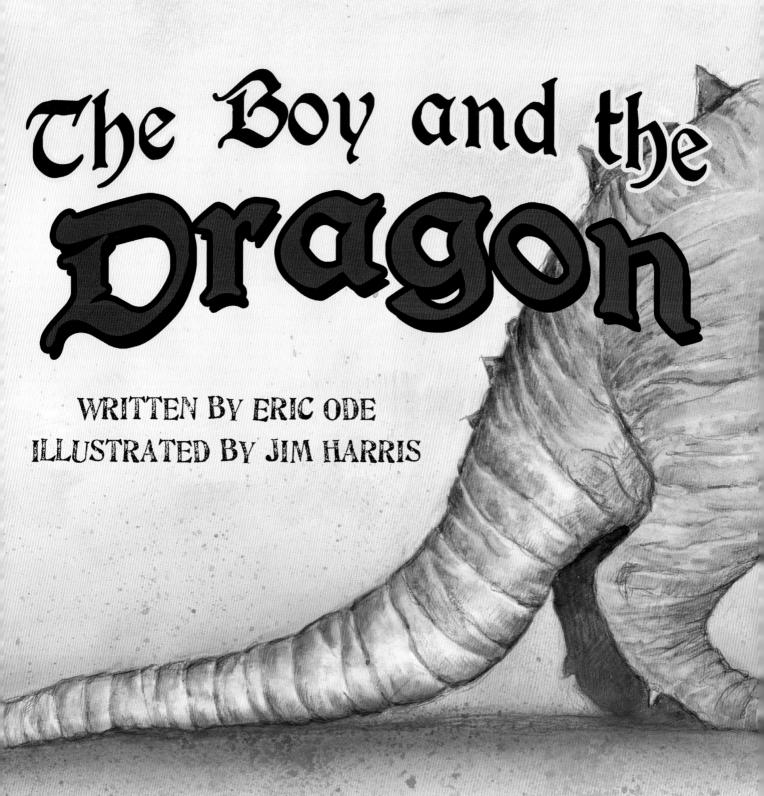

# The Boy and the Dragon

WRITTEN BY ERIC ODE
ILLUSTRATED BY JIM HARRIS

PELICAN PUBLISHING COMPANY
Gretna 2013

*To Tavin, strong, wise, and brave—E. O.*

*To Houston, fixer of gadgets and problem solver par excellence. If anybody could fix a dragon's wagon, you could.—J. H.*

*The word "Pelican" and the depiction of a pelican are trademarks of Pelican Publishing Company, Inc., and are registered in the U.S. Patent and Trademark Office.*

Library of Congress Cataloging-in-Publication Data

Ode, Eric.
  The boy and the dragon / by Eric Ode ; illustrated by Jim Harris.
      pages cm
  Summary: "Three knights and a boy travel east in search of a horrid and hideous beast. Is it the boy who finally succeeds in outwitting this dragon?"— Provided by publisher.
  ISBN 978-1-4556-1813-2 (hardcover : alk. paper) — ISBN 978-1-4556-1814-9 (e-book)
[1. Stories in rhyme. 2. Knights and knighthood—Fiction. 3. Courage—Fiction. 4. Dragons—Fiction.] I. Harris, Jim, 1955- illustrator. II. Title.
  PZ8.3.O277Bo 2013
  [E]—dc23
                                                                                    2012049162

Printed in Malaysia

Published by Pelican Publishing Company, Inc.
1000 Burmaster Street, Gretna, Louisiana 70053

**This** is the tale of three knights and a boy.
It's a thrilling adventure I think you'll enjoy.

Simon the Wise was the smartest of men.
Bogsworth the Strong had the power of ten.
Randolph the Brave led a life filled with glory.
And then there was Saul,
so quiet and small.
I guess you may wonder why *he's* in this story.

One cold autumn morning, these knights traveled east
in search of a horrid and hideous beast:
a green, scaly dragon with leathery wings
who gobbled up villagers, peasants, and kings.
And so, with a shout,
the three knights set out,
while Saul tagged along to carry their things.

Folks cheered and waved to these noble companions
as onward they traveled toward marshes and canyons.
Randolph the Brave, he lifted his chin
and shouted, "Hoorah! There's a battle to win!
We'll search high and low,
and we'll sing as we go!"
So Saul strummed along on an old mandolin.

*"We're three fearless knights!*
*We're strong, wise, and brave!*
*It's danger we seek—*
*it's adventure we crave!*
*That dragon had better*
*beware and behave.*
*We're three fearless knights!*
*Hoorah!"*

They marched through a valley. They hiked up a ridge.
And then, at a river, they came to a bridge.
There stood an old wizard, a beard to his knees,
and Randolph said, "Sir, step aside, if you please.
We're three fearless knights—we have places to go."
The old wizard scowled and said, "No."

"Perhaps," replied Randolph, "you'd move if you knew
I'm Randolph the Brave! I'm not frightened by *you.*"
"I see," said the wizard. "But how about this?"
And then, with a flash, and a pop, and a hiss,
that wizard turned into a great, beastly bear
with lightning-bright stripes in his blue, shaggy hair.

But Randolph said, "No, I'm not frightened of that."
So *poof* went the wizard—and there stood a rat,
a long-whiskered creature as big as a whale
with sharp, pointy claws and a fat, yellow tail.
But Randolph just smiled. He sighed, and he yawned.
The wizard grew puzzled, then *poof,* waved his wand,
and there stood an elephant six stories tall!
But Randolph the Brave wasn't frightened at all.

Then Saul said, "Brave Randolph, we can't wait all day.
We really must hurry and be on our way."
So onward they traveled, but brave Randolph stayed
to show that old wizard he wasn't afraid.
And as the two knights and the boy walked along,
Simon and Bogsworth burst into a song.

*"We're two fearless knights!*
*We're strong and we're wise!*
*We'll face any danger,*
*wherever it lies!*
*That dragon is in*
*for an awful surprise!*
*We're two fearless knights!*
*Hoorah!"*

They came to a forest—a dark, eerie place—
with branches and thickets that filled every space.
And Bogsworth said, "Here lies the end of our chase.
I think you'll agree
it is too dark to see.
I can't find my fingers in front of my face."

Simon just laughed, "I'll tell you, my friend,
I'm Simon the Wise, and this isn't the end.
I'm surely so bright, I don't need any light."
He entered the forest and vanished from sight.
And all they could hear was the sound of his boots
as he bumped into trees and tripped over the roots.

But Saul found a lamp and at once had it lit.
He whistled to Bogsworth, and so, bit by bit,
they trudged through that forest. Now two in the gang,
Bogsworth the Strong raised his sword as he sang,

*"I'm one fearless knight!*
*There's no one as strong!*
*I'll fight every fight.*
*I'll right every wrong!*
*That dragon will wish*
*I had not come along.*
*I'm one fearless knight!*
*Hoorah!"*

Just when they thought they'd left troubles behind,
they rounded a corner, and what did they find?
A round-headed ogre, a giant in size,
with boulder-like shoulders and tightly closed eyes.
Saul stepped up slowly, and as he was creeping,
he knew from the snoring, that ogre was sleeping.

Saul whispered to Bogsworth, "Let's tiptoe around him.
We'll leave that great creature to sleep where we found him."
"Nonsense," said Bogsworth, who chuckled at Saul.
"I'm Bogsworth the Strong! That would not do at all.
I'll move him aside. This should just take a nudge."
He pushed and he shoved, but that beast wouldn't budge.
He strained and he struggled—that knight wouldn't quit.
But still that great beast wouldn't budge, not a bit.

As Bogsworth continued to grunt and to groan,
Saul crept around them to travel alone.
He struck up a song while marching along:

*"I'm one little kid,*
*just me, and just one,*
*but still there's a dangerous*
*job to be done.*
*It seems this adventure*
*has only begun!*
*I'm one little kid.*
*Oh my!"*

Into the mountains, as brave as you please,
through branches that bent in the evening breeze,
he climbed to the top
and came to a stop,
for there stood the dragon, as tall as the trees.

He said to the boy with a great, gruesome sneer,
"You're small for a knight. What are you doing here?
I'll gobble you up in one lip-smacking bite!"
Saul simply said, "Yes, I guess that you might."

"But still," said the boy as he hatched up a plan,
"I've come here to fight you. I will, and I can.
Laugh if you wish, but I'm more than I seem:
I marched past the wizard who guarded the stream;
I walked through the forest where sunlight won't shine;
I strolled past the ogre—but me, I'm still fine."

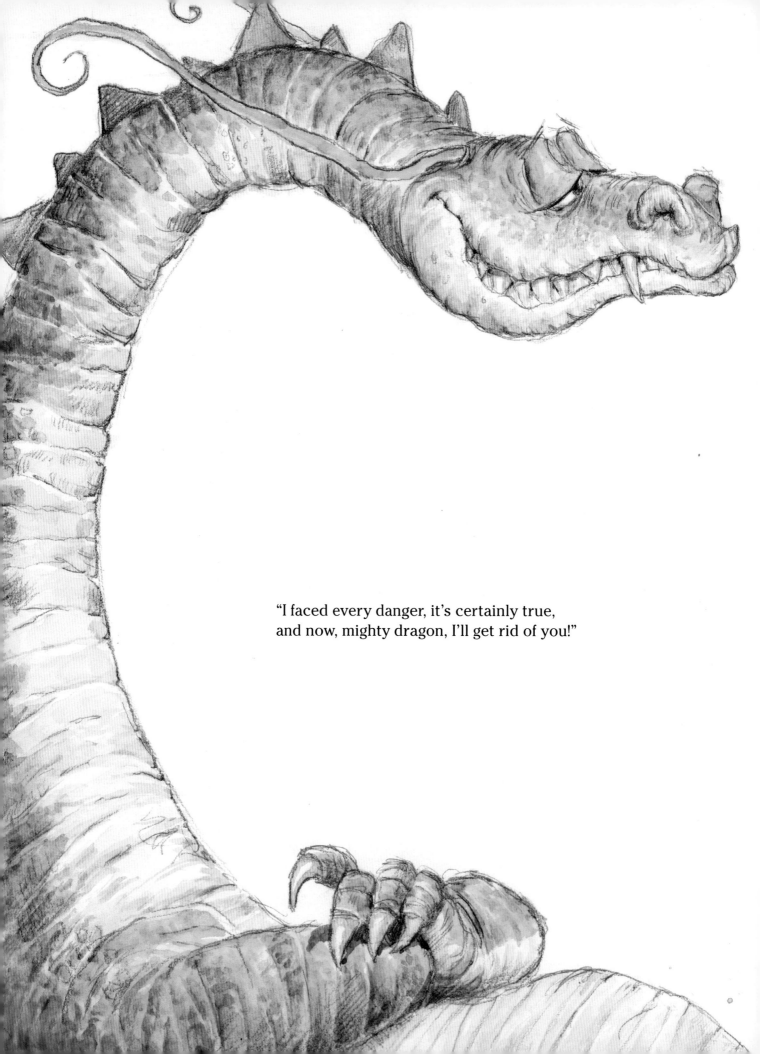

"I faced every danger, it's certainly true,
and now, mighty dragon, I'll get rid of you!"

"You see," said the boy, with a small, hopeful grin,
"There's magic at work in this old mandolin.
I'll play you a tune, and before you can blink,
you'll find, mighty dragon, you're starting to shrink.
You'll wither and shrivel and soon be so small,
that quickly you'll find you are nothing at all."

Then Saul played a tune with a plunk and a plink,
and soon that great beast didn't know what to think,
for Saul stood on tip-toes, and as he stood taller,
that dragon was certain *he* must have grown smaller.
"Stop!" said the beast with a howl and a roar.
"Not one little plink! Not a single plunk more!"

"I see it is true: you could shrink me with ease.
Oh, stop!" said the dragon. "No more, if you please!"
Saul gave a nod, and he smiled and said,
"Then off with you, dragon! It's time that you fled.
It's time you were banished and vanished from sight."
And so, like a shadow, that dragon took flight.
He soared from the mountain and into the night.

And never, not ever again was he seen,
that beast of a dragon, all scaly and green.
And as the stars shimmered, and as the moon shone,
that one noble knight traveled home all alone.